W9-BON-213

THE NATURAL

KICK!

THE NATURAL

CHRIS KREIE

MINNEAPOLIS

Darby Creek
A division of Lerner Publishing Group, Inc.
241 First Avenue North
Minneapolis, MN 55401 USA

For reading levels and more information, look up this title at
www.lernerbooks.com.

The images in this book are used with the permission of: iStockphoto.com/XiXinXing; iStockphoto.com/PhonlamaiPhoto; iStockphoto.com/Purdue9394; iStock.com/sumnersgraphicsinc.

Main body text set in Janson Text LT Std 12/17.5.
Typeface provided by Adobe Systems.

Library of Congress Cataloging-in-Publication Data

The Cataloging-in-Publication Data for *The Natural* is on file at the Library of Congress.
ISBN 978-1-5415-0019-8 (lib. bdg.)
ISBN 978-1-5415-0025-9 (pbk.)
ISBN 978-1-5415-0026-6 (eb pdf)

Manufactured in the United States of America
1-43651-33468-9/27/2017

KAMAL took the pass and dribbled along the sideline. His eyes were up, looking for an open teammate, but he couldn't find one. Everyone was covered. A defender dove in for the ball, but Kamal pushed it to his left foot and exploded past him. Kamal was in the open, moving toward the center of the field. He finally had some space to move.

Kamal was desperate to score. His team, the Panthers, was playing an away game against the Mountain View Miners. Midway through the second half, the Panthers were trailing 2–0.

Suddenly, two Miners defenders ran toward Kamal. He didn't think he could get around both of them—he would have to give up the ball. That's when he spotted his friend and teammate, Rodrigo, open on the other side of the field. Kamal and Rodrigo were the team's best forwards, and they'd been playing together since middle school. Kamal had a powerful right foot, and Rodrigo was deadly with his left. Together they were almost impossible to stop.

Kamal cocked his right leg and sent a crossing pass to Rodrigo. Rodrigo protected the ball from his defender then quickly fired a pass back to Kamal, who was moving toward the penalty box in front of the goal. Kamal caught the ball in stride and pushed forward.

Another defender rushed toward him. Kamal stopped, trapping the ball with his right foot. As the defender slowed down to keep pace, Kamal sped around him.

Kamal was just a few steps from the box. He eyed the goalie, who was in good position with his knees bent and his arms stretched out low at his sides. But Kamal quickly found an opening. The goalie was leaving a little room to his right. Kamal fired. The ball shot off his foot, staying close to the ground. The goalie kicked out his right leg, but he couldn't reach it. The ball sailed past him and streaked into the back of the goal.

His teammates rushed toward him in celebration. "Nice play," said Rodrigo. "Perfect give-and-go. Way to finish."

"Great job finding me," said Kamal as they jogged toward the other end of the field.

Rodrigo smiled. "I know your moves before you make them."

"That's right," said Kamal. "And without you, a lot of those moves wouldn't be possible."

They shared a high five. "Let's get another one, Big Dog," said Rodrigo.

Big Dog was Rodrigo's nickname for Kamal. He called him that because Kamal was the best player on the team. The captain, the alpha dog. Kamal wasn't sure he loved the nickname, but it did make him feel more powerful on the field.

The teams lined up for the kickoff. Kamal loved the thrill of scoring a goal, but he had to put it behind him and focus on the next one.

The Miners were still ahead by one and the game was nearing the end. He wondered if his team would have time to come back.

The Panthers needed a win. They had already lost the first two games of the season. The last thing Kamal wanted was to make it 0–3. He wanted this year, his senior season, to be a great one for the Panthers. He had hopes of winning the conference and maybe even making it to State. Another loss could put those goals out of reach.

The Miners began moving up the field toward the Panthers' goal. Mountain View was a precise team. A team that made quick, short passes and was content to control the ball for long stretches of time. They were extremely patient. This type of play was frustrating for Kamal and his teammates because it prevented them from playing with the aggressive style they preferred. Instead, they had to wait for opportunities. If the Panthers' defense attacked at the wrong time, the Miners would pounce on that mistake and make them pay.

That's just what happened next. As the Miners passed the ball back and forth, one of the Panthers grew restless. He made a break on the ball, attempting to intercept a pass. But he missed the ball and put himself out of position. That was all the space the Miners needed. They quickly moved toward midfield, dancing between defenders and making short, accurate passes.

Kamal stayed locked on the player he was defending and watched the action unfold in front of him. He desperately wanted to run in and attack the ball, but he didn't want to leave the player he was defending in case the pass went his way. He needed to have faith in his teammates and stay patient.

The rest happened in a flash. One of the Miners finally kicked a deep ball. He lofted a pass into the box, catching the Panthers by surprise. It landed at the feet of a Miners forward who collected it and crossed the ball to a teammate in the opposite corner. He finished the job, sending the ball screaming past the goalie and into the net.

It turned out to be the last goal of the game. Moments later the referee blew his whistle, ending a 3–1 victory for the Miners.

After the game, Kamal and Rodrigo sat in the grass, watching the Miners celebrate their win.

"I can barely remember what it feels like to win," said Rodrigo.

"Same here," said Kamal. He shook his head. "Three games and already three losses. Not how I thought the season would begin."

"Three games and only three goals," said Rodrigo. "You and I are the only players who have scored."

"I know," said Kamal. "Some of the other guys need to step up, or this season's just going to get worse."

Rodrigo popped to his feet. "We're a young team," he said. "Don't give up on the guys just yet." He reached his hand down to Kamal.

Kamal grabbed it and let Rodrigo help him to his feet. "If you say so," said Kamal. "All I know is this team better turn things around. And fast."

KAMAL and Rodrigo met up the next day in physics. It was Kamal's favorite class of the day. He gave his friend a fist bump as he sat down. "What's up?"

"The ceiling, the sky, and Mr. Nguyen's IQ," said Rodrigo. "Are you going to get him today?"

Kamal laughed. "We'll see."

When Mr. Nguyen entered the classroom, Kamal said, "Morning, Mr. Nguyen! You ready for Fun Physics Friday?"

Mr. Nguyen laughed. "Of course. What's the question today?"

Kamal had a knack for physics, and he liked to show it off. Every Friday, he would try to stump Mr. Nguyen with a question. The teacher almost always played along, which was one of the reasons Kamal liked him so much.

"OK. This man is known as the father of quantum theory. Who is he?"

"Albert Einstein!" shouted Rodrigo. Some of the students laughed.

"Wrong," said Kamal.

"Hmm, the father of quantum theory," said Mr. Nguyen, playing along. "Can you give me a hint? Was he a pirate, perhaps?"

Kamal was confused. "As far as I know he was just a physicist. I didn't read anything about him being a pirate."

"Well, I think he was a pirate," said Mr. Nguyen. "And I think he once even had to walk the . . ." He paused dramatically.

Kamal rolled his eyes and smiled. Mr. Nguyen knew the answer. He always knew the answer.

"Plank!" shouted Mr. Nguyen. "Max Planck was the father of quantum theory. Am I right?"

"Of course you're right," said Kamal. Rodrigo and a few others laughed. As corny as this routine was, the students appreciated a lighthearted start to the day.

Suddenly a student walked through the classroom door. He was tall, with perfectly combed blond hair. Kamal had never seen him before. The rest of the students went silent.

"Can I help you?" asked Mr. Nguyen.

"I hope so." The boy smiled, showing off deep dimples. Some of the girls whispered to one another. "Is this physics? Are you Mr. Nguyen?"

Kamal could hear the girls behind him. "He's so cute," one of them said.

"Yes," said Mr. Nguyen. "You must be Justin. It's your first day with us, right?"

"That's right," said Justin.

"Well, welcome to Ridgeview High," said Mr. Nguyen. "Take any open seat."

Justin walked down a row of desks. He nodded and smiled at several students before sitting down.

"We have a tradition in my class of greeting new students with a few friendly questions," said Mr. Nguyen. "Justin, are you game?"

"Of course," said Justin.

"I'll start things out," said Mr. Nguyen. "What's your favorite subject in school?"

"Science," said Justin. "Physics, actually."

Kamal leaned toward Rodrigo. "What a suck-up," he said under his breath. Rodrigo chuckled.

"Good answer," said Mr. Nguyen.

"No, really," said Justin. "I'm not just saying that. I love physics. We did a lab at my old school about the coefficient of friction just before I left. It was amazing."

Kamal frowned. *Justin might know more about physics than I do*, he thought.

"Great," said Mr. Nguyen. "OK, next question."

"Where are you from?" asked a girl in the front row.

"I'm from the great state of California," said Justin. "Home of the Pacific Ocean, the Sierra Nevada mountains, and the coolest people in the world. Specifically, I'm from San Diego."

"What a weirdo," Kamal whispered. This time Rodrigo ignored him. The rest of the students seemed fascinated by the new guy.

"Did you surf in California?" asked one of the girls.

"Of course," said Justin. "I carved up the waves whenever I could."

"Have you met any famous celebrities?" asked another girl.

"Actually, yeah," said Justin. "My uncle works at a movie studio in LA. He brings me to the set when I visit him. I've even helped the crew set up equipment for movies. It's pretty sweet."

Kamal looked around the room. All eyes were glued to Justin. *This guy knows how to make a first impression*, he thought. Justin's charm and good looks had captivated everyone, especially the girls. And his knowledge of physics seemed to have impressed Mr. Nguyen. He had brains to go along with his cute smile.

"All right," said Mr. Nguyen. "Time for physics. Everyone open to page sixty-one in your textbooks."

After physics, Kamal and Rodrigo packed up their stuff and walked into the hallway together. Justin was already there, chatting with one of the girls from class.

"Excuse me," he said to the girl, and then he walked up to Kamal and Rodrigo. "Hey! I'm Justin."

"Rodrigo." He patted his chest. "And this is Kamal."

"Great to meet you guys," said Justin. "Question for you. You guys look pretty fit. Are you athletes?"

What an awkward question, thought Kamal.

"We play soccer," said Rodrigo.

"I knew it," said Justin, a big smile on his face. "I can tell."

"You must play sports too," said Rodrigo.

If anyone looked like an athlete, it was Justin. He was tall and lean with broad shoulders. Kamal could see well-defined muscles bulging under his tight T-shirt.

"Lacrosse," said Justin. "That was my game back in San Diego."

Kamal remained silent. Feeling uncomfortable, he pulled out his phone so he'd have something to do.

"Ridgeview has a lacrosse team," said Rodrigo.

"I know," said Justin. "But I hear they don't play in the fall, just the spring."

"That's true," said Rodrigo.

"I need something to do now," said Justin. "I'm restless, and I need to stay in shape."

"Well," said Rodrigo. "You could do football or cross-country." He paused. "Or you could come out for soccer. Do you play?"

Kamal looked up from his phone. *Did Rodrigo really just invite this hotshot to join the soccer team?* he thought.

Justin laughed. "Not since elementary school."

"You should try it," said Rodrigo. He seemed excited about the idea. "Coach Hayes never cuts players. Not all of the guys play much, but everyone who wants to join gets a spot on the team. So even if you're rusty and don't get into games, you'll get a great workout in practice. We go hard."

"Cool, I'll think about it." The next bell rang. Justin lightly punched Rodrigo in the shoulder. "Thanks for the invite, Rodrigo. Maybe I'll see you out there after school."

"See ya."

"Kamal." Justin nodded at him.

"Later," said Kamal.

They watched Justin disappear into a sea of students.

Kamal turned to Rodrigo. "What did you do that for?"

"What?"

Kamal pretended to be Rodrigo. "You should, like, join soccer, bro. It would be, like, totally cool to have you on the team, dude."

"I did not sound like that," said Rodrigo.

"Oh, really?" Kamal smiled.

"You have a problem with Justin?" asked Rodrigo as the two of them began to walk to their next class.

"I don't have a problem with him," said Kamal. "But you heard what he said. He hasn't played soccer in years."

"I don't think Justin will do anything to hurt the team, if that's what you're worried about," said Rodrigo.

"He certainly won't help," said Kamal. "My focus is on the guys who produce, the guys who actually contribute. I'm thinking of the team. I want us to get better and finally win a game. You think bringing in someone who hasn't played since elementary school is going to improve things?"

"Maybe," said Rodrigo, shrugging. "Besides, if he's no good, he won't even play in the games. No big deal." Kamal didn't answer. He wasn't sure how to explain that this *did* seem like a big deal to him.

KAMAL and Rodrigo sat together on the soccer field. Practice was about to start, and they were going through their normal stretching routine.

Justin was in the middle of the field, talking with a few guys from the team. "He actually showed up," said Rodrigo. "I wasn't sure he would."

"He's wasting his time—and ours." Kamal stretched both legs straight out in front of him and reached his hands forward. "This team needs to get better, not worse. Having Justin here is not going to help us get our first win of the season."

"Give the guy a chance," said Rodrigo. "Everyone seems to like him. He might not help us on the field, but maybe he'll be good for morale."

"We'll see." Kamal let out a chuckle. "He looks like a clown." Justin was wearing old cleats he must've scavenged from a box in the locker room, and his borrowed shorts were about two sizes too small. His long legs seemed to stretch for miles. To cap it off, the flimsy, neon-green pads that he'd wrapped around his shins seemed more for decoration than for protection. "I think I wore shin guards like that when I was five. My mom bought them for me at the dollar store."

"Aw, come on, man," said Rodrigo, shaking his head but giving a little chuckle.

None of the other players focused on Justin's outfit. They were chatting with him, laughing, and having a good time. Kamal's teammates were welcoming him with open arms.

Suddenly a whistle blew. It was Coach Hayes, standing on the end line near one of the goals.

Kamal jumped to his feet and raced across

the field to join his coach. Rodrigo and the other players followed his lead.

"Bring it in, fellas," said Coach Hayes. Everyone gathered in front of him. "Before we get started, I want us to acknowledge our new teammate. Justin, welcome aboard."

Justin nodded and smiled. "Thanks, Coach Hayes. Happy to be here."

"Let's hear it for him, everyone." The team applauded, and a couple of the guys clapped Justin on the back. Kamal couldn't have clapped any less enthusiastically.

"All right, guys," said Coach Hayes. "Line it up. Two lines." The players shuffled toward the end line, coming together in two separate lines. Kamal was at the head of one line. Rodrigo was at the head of the other. Stretched out on the ground in front of each of them was a long agility ladder.

"Two steps in to the left!" yelled Coach Hayes. "As quick as you can. Ready?" Kamal leaned forward. "Go!"

Kamal's feet moved like lightning. He sprinted into the ladder and then back out in a flash. He repeated the steps twelve times as he progressed swiftly and perfectly through each rung, never slowing down. Rodrigo stepped through the ladder next to Kamal's, but he couldn't keep up. Kamal finished ahead of him.

"Next!" yelled Coach Hayes. "Go!" Two new players took their turns in the drill, then two more and two more until the only players left were Justin and a sophomore forward.

"Justin, you get the drill?" asked Coach Hayes.

"I've got it," Justin said confidently.

"All right," said Coach Hayes. "Go!"

Justin raced forward. Kamal watched with curiosity. *Let's see what this guy can do*, he thought. Justin made it successfully through the first two rungs, but on the third one his feet tangled together and he went crashing to the ground.

I guess he can't do much.

Justin got right back up and continued.

"Take your time!" barked Coach Hayes. "It's not easy to get the footwork right the first time. Keep going. You'll get it!"

Justin continued, moving more slowly to

make sure he got the moves right. "That's it!" shouted Rodrigo.

Justin completed the ladder in about twice the time it had taken everyone else. "Nice try, California," Kamal said. "Soccer's not so easy, is it?"

"Go easy on him, Big Dog," said Rodrigo.

Kamal shot him a confused look. *Why should I go easy on this new guy when I don't go easy on any of my actual teammates? Not to mention myself. Justin should be held to the same standard as the rest of us.*

"Again!" demanded Coach Hayes.

The team did the same ladder drill several more times. Kamal smoked every player he faced. Justin, much to Kamal's surprise, quickly got better. He even began winning some of his matchups.

"Great work, Justin!" shouted Coach Hayes. "All right, last one!"

Justin and Kamal stood in opposite lines, waiting for players in front of them to finish the drill. "Big Dog, is it?" Justin asked.

Kamal looked over. Justin had a smirk on his face. "You talking to me?" asked Kamal.

"You are the Big Dog, aren't you?" asked Justin. "What do you say—me and you this time? Head to head?"

Kamal laughed. "You serious?"

"You scared?" asked Justin.

"In your dreams." He was confident. He'd show Justin exactly why his teammates called him the Big Dog. "All right. Your funeral." Justin exchanged spots with the player in front of him.

Kamal and Justin stood at the front of the lines.

"Ready?" shouted Coach Hayes. Kamal leaned forward and put his game face on. "Go!"

They shot toward the ladders.

Kamal realized his mistake about halfway through the ladder. He was moving more slowly than normal. He was focusing on the steps instead of letting his body just flow through the ladder like it normally did. He was thinking too much. He tried to speed up at the sixth rung, but then he almost tripped on the seventh. He could see Justin out of the corner of his eye. The new guy was keeping up.

Kamal moved awkwardly through the eighth rung, then the ninth. He was almost there. Just three rungs to go. He could hear the cheering of his teammates. Tenth rung. Eleventh. He felt like his feet might get tangled up at any moment. He fought his way through the final rung, lunged forward, and looked to his left. Justin had finished a step ahead of him.

"And the new guy wins!" shouted Rodrigo.

Kamal bent over to catch his breath. He couldn't believe he had lost. Justin walked over and reached out his arm. "Nice run, Big Dog," he said. "You almost had me."

Coach Hayes announced the next drill before Kamal could respond. "Partner push-ups!" he commanded.

Kamal grabbed Justin's outstretched hand, stood tall, and looked him in the eyes. "Rematch?" he said.

"OK," said Justin with a smile. "You're on."

Kamal was a beast at push-ups. Partner

push-ups was a drill the team did almost every practice, and he always crushed it.

The players went down to their stomachs to prepare for the push-ups. They lay an arm's length away from their partner in front of them.

Kamal tried to stare down Justin. Justin didn't blink.

"Ready . . . go!" shouted Coach Hayes.

The players began the drill. They did regular push-ups, but each time they pushed their bodies off the ground, they reached an arm out in front of them, slapping the hand of their partner. The players continued this way, switching hands each time, for as long as their arms could take it.

Kamal went fast. "Think you can keep up, rookie?" he asked.

The two slapped hands. "Not a problem," said Justin.

The push-ups continued. Before long, players around Kamal began dropping to the ground from exhaustion. Two groups dropped out, then five, then eight. Soon the only guys still doing push-ups were Kamal and Justin.

Everyone else sat in the grass, breathing hard and looking on.

"Let's go, Kamal!" yelled Rodrigo.

"Tired yet?" asked Justin.

Kamal didn't want to admit it, but he was definitely getting tired. He was slowing down and he knew that Justin had noticed.

Justin was a machine. He barely seemed to be sweating. Kamal knew he wouldn't be able to keep up for long.

Justin put on the pressure. He began to speed up.

"Great effort, guys!" shouted Coach Hayes.

Kamal pushed and pushed and pushed. His arms were like rubber. He knew they would give out any second. Finally, they did. He did one last push-up and then collapsed onto the field, his face buried deep in the grass.

A cheer went out from the team. Kamal wasn't sure if they were cheering for the show or if some of his teammates were happy Justin won.

Kamal lay on his stomach, exhausted. Justin stood up and patted him on the back.

"Good effort, Big Dog," he said. "Don't feel bad. I do push-ups in my sleep. Nobody back in San Diego could beat me. You never had a chance." He walked away.

Kamal couldn't move. His arms burned as he sucked in huge gulps of air, and he knew he would probably be sore tomorrow. But even worse, his pride was wounded.

"HE'S a natural," said Rodrigo as he
and Kamal gulped water on the sideline.
Kamal was still picking up the pieces of his
shattered ego.

"He's cocky," said Kamal. "And a showboat."

"I like him," said Rodrigo.

"He's fast and he's strong," said Kamal. "I'll
give him that much."

"You said he was going to make the team
worse." Rodrigo laughed. "Feel like changing
that statement now?"

"Anybody can run fast and do push-ups,"
said Kamal. "Let's see how he does with
a ball."

"Everybody, back on the field!" barked
Coach Hayes.

"You don't like him much do you?" asked Rodrigo.

"What on Earth gave you that idea?" asked Kamal dryly.

Rodrigo smiled. "Could Big Dog be intimidated by the new dog?"

Kamal didn't have a chance to respond before Rodrigo jogged back onto the field. Throwing his water bottle on the ground, Kamal ran toward his teammates.

Coach Hayes was ready with the next set of drills. "Triangle. Three cones, three players, two balls. Group up!"

"Kamal! Join us!" It was Rodrigo, standing next to Justin. Kamal rolled his eyes.

The triangle drill required footwork and speed, and Kamal loved it. Rodrigo explained the drill to Justin. "Kamal will go first. You and I will feed him balls as he does various skills around the cones. You'll get it."

"Let's do it," said Justin.

Three cones were set up in a triangle, each one about eight feet apart. Kamal stood outside of the triangle between two of the cones.

Rodrigo and Justin stood near the other cone, the tip of the triangle. Each of them had a ball and faced Kamal.

Rodrigo began the drill by passing his ball to Kamal. Kamal immediately kicked it back, shuffled to the inside of the cone on his left, got the next pass from Rodrigo, and kicked it back. He then danced sideways to the inside of the other cone. Justin kicked his ball to him, but it missed by several feet and sailed past Kamal.

Kamal shook his head as he ran to retrieve it.

"That's all right," said Rodrigo to Justin. "You'll get it."

Kamal set up again on the outside of the triangle. "Let's go," he said.

Justin kicked the ball. Kamal received it, kicked it back, and then broke right. Justin attempted to kick it back to him in rhythm, but again he missed with his pass. Kamal had to stretch out for the ball and move out of position.

Kamal dribbled back to the outside of the triangle. He looked at Justin. "Are you ready this time, California?" he asked.

"Ready," said Justin.

"Are you sure?" asked Kamal. "Because I can slow down if you want."

"Just give me the ball, funny man," said Justin.

They started the drill, but again Justin screwed up the pass, this time kicking it too hard and over Kamal's head.

Kamal looked back at him. "My foot's down here." He stuck out his right leg.

"He's trying," said Rodrigo. "Give him a break."

The drill continued the same way for the next several minutes. Justin could not get the timing right. Almost all his passes missed their mark.

Eventually Coach Hayes jogged over. "Switch this out, guys," he said. "Justin, I want you to work with me. Kamal and Rodrigo, find another third to join your group."

"You'll get it," Rodrigo told Justin as he walked away. "Just keep working."

"Or just stick to lacrosse," said Kamal under his breath.

"I still think he could help the team once he figures things out," said Rodrigo.

"Help us get water at halftime, maybe," said Kamal.

As they continued the triangle drill with a different teammate, Kamal kept one eye on Justin and Coach Hayes. Justin seemed to be getting frustrated. His footwork was a mess and he was having a hard time making even the easiest of passes back to his coach.

Minutes later, Coach Hayes was ready for the next drill. "Attack and defend!" he shouted. He had two small goals set up in the middle of the field about thirty feet away from each other. "Two teams. Line it up!"

The drill was simple. The player at the front of one line dribbled forward and attempted to score a goal. The player from the other line defended.

Kamal was first to try to score. "Go!" shouted Coach Hayes. Kamal darted forward. As his defender approached, Kamal shifted the ball back and forth between his feet. He faked left, moved right, then paused before bursting to the right, catching his defender off guard and moving around him. He dribbled forward and drilled the ball into the goal. "Great moves!" shouted Coach Hayes. "Next up!"

Kamal watched his teammates take their turns. Then Justin was up. He tentatively dribbled the ball forward. His defender quickly closed on the ball, poked his left foot at it, and stole it away. Justin was flatfooted as the other player collected the ball and went for the easy score in the other direction.

Kamal shook his head. *This is a waste of time*, he thought.

"Nice try, Justin!" shouted Coach Hayes. "Protect the ball next time." Justin ran to the end of the line.

Soon Kamal was back at the front of the line. This time he was defending. He easily outplayed his opponent and tackled the ball away, clearing it off the field.

As the drill went on, players kept easily dribbling around Justin during every matchup.

Finally it was the moment Kamal had been waiting for. He faced off against Justin, and this time he was sure he would beat him.

Kamal had the ball. He smiled across the field at his opponent.

Justin smiled back. "Let's do this," he said. "Show me what you've got."

Kamal couldn't believe Justin was talking smack, especially after the way he'd been performing so far. "I'm coming for you, California," he said.

Kamal had no intention of messing around. He didn't just want to score on Justin, he wanted to humiliate him. He wanted to get back at Justin for beating him in the ladder drill and the push-up challenge earlier in practice. "Time to go back to lacrosse."

"Go!" shouted Coach Hayes.

Kamal exploded forward. Normally he was cautious in this drill, dribbling carefully and protecting the ball from the defender, making sure it wasn't tackled away. But this was different. He didn't have to be worried with Justin. He didn't have to be careful. All he had to do was stick with the fundamentals and he'd be able to beat him easily.

He dribbled toward Justin. Just as it looked like Kamal was about to crash directly into him, Kamal burst to his left. Justin was a statue. Kamal spun his body, twirled around with the ball, then blasted past Justin. He dribbled slowly the rest of the way and nudged the ball into the goal.

Some of the players hooted and hollered.

"Great footwork, Kamal!" shouted Coach Hayes.

"I'll get you next time," said Justin.

Kamal laughed. "Whatever you say."

Kamal joined his teammates in line and smiled. His earlier worries about Justin showing him up were a thing of the past. The guy was strong and fast, but on the soccer field, Kamal was, and forever would be, the Big Dog.

ON Saturday, Kamal tried to get in touch with Rodrigo several times, but Rodrigo didn't pick up his phone or answer his texts.

Finally, Rodrigo responded with a text that night: *Hey. What's up?*

Want to kick the ball around tomorrow? Kamal texted back.

Can't. I'm going to my cousin's birthday party. See you Monday.

So instead of practicing with his friend, Kamal decided to spend the day doing some conditioning. He lifted weights in his garage, then spent the afternoon on a ten-mile run.

Kamal felt strong and confident at school on Monday morning. "Let's get started, everyone," said Mr. Nguyen as the bell rang for physics class. Students settled into their chairs.

"How was your weekend, Mr. Nguyen?" Kamal asked, winking at Rodrigo. Kamal loved Mr. Nguyen. But as much as Kamal enjoyed the class, it was even more fun to send Mr. Nguyen off on a tangent. Mr. Nguyen loved telling stories, and it was easy to get him distracted.

"I went sky diving!" said Mr. Nguyen. "Can you believe it? Your humble physics teacher jumped out of an airplane at ten thousand feet! What a rush! Have any of you ever done it?"

Justin raised his hand. *Of course*, thought Kamal. He rolled his eyes.

"I have," said Justin. "It's the best, isn't it? Did you do tandem or solo?"

"Tandem, of course," said Mr. Nguyen. "It was my first time."

"Tandem is awesome," said Justin. "But I do solo now."

"I would love to go solo," said Mr. Nguyen. "Let's talk after class. Maybe you can give me some advice."

"Sure thing, Mr. Nguyen."

Kamal couldn't believe what was happening. *Justin's already screwed things up on the soccer field,* he thought. *Now it's like he wants to become best friends with my favorite teacher.*

"But, oh, that feeling of stepping out of the plane and just falling through the air," said Mr. Nguyen. "So amazing."

"I know, right?" said Justin. "I bet you were calculating the physics of skydiving while you were up there."

"How did you guess?" More laughter.

Kamal made a disgusted noise under his breath.

"Did you say something, Kamal?" asked Mr. Nguyen.

Justin chuckled. "He doesn't like me very much."

"Whatever," said Kamal.

Justin continued. "I beat him in some soccer drills on Friday. Kamal doesn't handle losing very well."

"And I beat you in the ones that counted," said Kamal sitting up straight in his chair.

"The ones where you actually had to kick a soccer ball."

"Ooh," said a few of the guys in the room.

"You're right," said Justin. "You did. But we'll see how things go in practice today, am I right Rodrigo?" He turned to Rodrigo.

Rodrigo put a hand over his face and slumped in his chair. Kamal gave him a confused look.

"All right, guys," said Mr. Nguyen. "Let's leave all that on the soccer field. There will be no trash-talking or macho chest-thumping in my classroom." He began to take things out of the box on his desk. "It's time for our lab. Everybody come gather around. Let's go."

Students got out of their seats and walked to the front of the room. Kamal turned to Rodrigo. "What was Justin talking about? 'We'll see how things go in practice today?' What's that supposed to mean?"

"I'll tell you later," said Rodrigo.

SPRINTS and conditioning drills at practice that afternoon went about the same way they had on Friday. Kamal tried his best, but on many of the drills he just couldn't keep up with Justin. The guy was unbeatable. Kamal had never seen a better natural athlete.

"Good try, Kamal," Justin said, grinning. "Nice effort. Keep up the hard work and you just might beat me one day!"

Kamal was okay with Justin's trash-talking in warm-ups. He knew that once the soccer balls came out, he would dominate again in the aspects of soccer that really mattered.

"Triangle!" shouted Coach Hayes after a short water break. "Groups of three!" It was the same drill they had done on Friday.

"Kamal!" said Justin as the team jogged toward the cones. "You, me, and Rodrigo?"

"Really?" asked Kamal. "Think you can actually do it this time?"

"Oh, I'm pretty sure I can do it." Kamal saw Justin wink at Rodrigo. Something was clearly up between them.

"All right," Kamal said. "But we're going full speed."

"Sounds good to me," said Justin.

"And if you kick the ball over my head again you're finding another group," said Kamal.

They set up at one of the sets of cones. "You want to go first?" Justin asked Kamal.

"I'm ready when you are." Kamal positioned himself on the outside of the right cone. He took a couple quick breaths and then started the drill. He kicked the ball to Justin then moved inside the cones. Justin made a perfect pass back to him. Kamal kicked it back then moved to the other cone. Rodrigo fed him the ball. He kicked it, moved around the cone, received the pass once again from Rodrigo, and passed it back to him. He then shuffled to the other side. Justin served him another perfect pass. Kamal returned the ball to him, moved to the outside of the cone, and got another great pass from Justin. The drill continued like this for the next several minutes. Not once did Justin make a bad pass to Kamal.

"Switch!" shouted Coach Hayes.

"Not too bad, huh, Kamal?" Justin asked.

Kamal traded spots with him. He was confused. Justin was about a hundred times better at the drill than he was last Friday. How was that possible?

Justin stood outside the right cone, a ball at his foot. "Let's do this." He kicked it to Kamal and then danced inside the cones. Kamal kicked it back. Justin moved to the next cone. He and Rodrigo traded passes while Justin stepped from inside the cones to the outside then back again. His timing was good. And the majority of his passes were crisp, sharp, and on target. He moved back to Kamal's side. Kamal fed him passes, watching Justin's clean footwork. *Who is this guy?* thought Kamal. *How in the world did he improve so much in just a couple of days?*

After several minutes, Coach Hayes shouted again. "Switch!"

As Justin traded places with Rodrigo, they shared a high five. "That's what I'm talking about! This soccer stuff isn't so hard, am I right, Kamal?"

Rodrigo took his turn. Once again Justin was dead on with his passes. Rodrigo eased through the drill with precision.

Coach Hayes was ready with the next exercise. "Everybody, over here!" he shouted.

The players jogged toward one of the goal's. Kamal stopped Rodrigo. "How did Justin get so good at that drill?" he asked him.

Rodrigo looked away.

"What are you not telling me?" asked Kamal.

Rodrigo looked back at him. "We worked out together on Saturday."

"You what?"

"Justin and I worked out together," said Rodrigo. "He asked me, so I helped him with a bunch of the drills and with his footwork and stuff."

"So that's why you weren't answering my texts," said Kamal.

"I didn't think you'd want to join us," said Rodrigo. "I know you don't like the guy."

"You've got that right," said Kamal. He shook his head. "Why in the world do you want to help Justin?"

"Why not?" asked Rodrigo. "He's a decent guy once you get to know him. And he's part of the team now. I want us to get better. I want us to go to State. Just like you, right?"

"Of course I want to go to State," said Kamal. "But Justin's not going to help us do that. Besides, the guy is such a showboat."

"It takes one to know one." Rodrigo smiled and smacked Kamal on the shoulder. "The competition will be good for you."

TUESDAY was game day. The Panthers were at home taking on the Birch Valley Buffaloes. The sun was shining, and a cool breeze was blowing down from the mountains and gently across the soccer field. It was a perfect day for soccer. Even Justin's presence on the team couldn't spoil that for Kamal.

He did a few standing stretches on the field as the Buffaloes prepared for the kickoff. Kamal looked to the stands. A group of girls he recognized from Ridgeview were taking their seats in the bleachers. Kamal didn't remember seeing them at a game before. Then he thought about Justin and shook his head. They must be here to see him.

"Let's go, everyone!" Kamal shouted, trying to get his mind off Justin and back on the game where it belonged.

"Play hard!" yelled Coach Hayes from the sidelines. "Start strong!"

Justin was standing next to Coach Hayes. Even with his quick improvement over the past couple of days, there was no way Coach Hayes was going to put him in the lineup. He had no clue how to position himself on the field, how to play team defense, or how to fit into the Panthers' offense. That meant game days were going to give Kamal a much-needed break from Justin.

The Buffaloes were a good team but not great. Kamal remembered beating them the previous year, 3–2. They were a good matchup for the Panthers. A team they needed to take seriously, but a team they could beat. The Panthers could hopefully defeat the Buffaloes and then begin their march to a conference title.

After controlling the ball for the first minute or so, the Buffaloes turned it over at midfield. Rodrigo pounced on it and cleared

the ball back to the Panthers' defense. Kamal
began jogging slowly along the near sideline
toward the Buffaloes goal. His teammates
behind him passed the ball back and forth,
moving bit by bit up the field.

Rodrigo raised his hand in the middle of
the field. He had gotten free from his defender,
and a Panthers teammate saw him and hit him
with a clean pass.

As several defenders converged on Rodrigo,
Kamal saw his chance. He sprinted toward the
left corner of the box, a spot that had been left
open by a Buffaloes defender who had moved
up to play Rodrigo. "Open!" he shouted.

Rodrigo spotted him and quickly passed
him the ball. "Go!" shouted Kamal the instant
Rodrigo had kicked the ball.

Rodrigo cleared himself from the defense
and bolted into the box. Kamal kicked it right
back to him, leading his friend toward the goal.
The timing was perfect. Rodrigo got to the
ball and immediately fired a shot. It looked
like a sure goal, but the Buffaloes goalie made
a stellar play on the ball, diving to his left and

getting just enough of his fingertips on it to send it wide and across the end line.

So close! Kamal put his hands to his head. Rodrigo looked back at him and applauded the assist attempt. Kamal gave him a thumbs-up. "Great run!" he shouted.

"Nice feed!" yelled Rodrigo.

Rodrigo's near miss turned out to be the best shot the Panthers got in the first half. After lots of back and forth with no further scoring opportunities for either team, the game was scoreless at halftime.

Things didn't change much in the second half. The Panthers' goalie had to turn away a couple nice shot attempts by the Buffaloes, but Kamal, Rodrigo, and his teammates just couldn't break the Buffaloes' defense. They were a wall, preventing the Panthers from getting anywhere near their goal.

With just a few minutes to go, Kamal received a pass and began to make a run along the near sideline. A Buffaloes player rushed over and slid, tackling the ball out of bounds. As Kamal went to retrieve it for a throw-in, he heard the referee's whistle. "Sub!" shouted the ref.

Kamal looked to the bench. He had to blink a few times to make sure he was really seeing what he thought he was seeing. Standing next to Coach Hayes and ready to come into the game was Justin. The referee waved him in and Justin ran onto the field to take the place of a teammate. The girls in the stands stood up and cheered. Kamal couldn't believe it.

Justin clearly wasn't ready to play in a game. He looked around nervously—he didn't even know where to go. "Take the middle!" Rodrigo shouted, pointing to a spot near the middle circle.

Kamal waited for Justin to get into position before throwing the ball to a teammate in the backfield. His teammate secured the ball then kicked it wide to a teammate on the right. Kamal jogged toward the Buffaloes' goal.

The Panthers passed the ball back and forth, moving slowly up the field. With only moments left in the game, Kamal knew this might be their final opportunity to end the scoreless deadlock.

Finally, the ball came back to him. Kamal collected it and glanced up. His defender was giving him some space. Kamal surveyed the players and saw that Rodrigo and Justin were both moving slowly in the middle of the field toward the box.

Kamal made up his mind. It was now or never. He took one last look at his defender and made his move. Kamal blasted past him to the left, just barely avoiding the defender's tackle. Then he was free. He dribbled forward, moving fast and doing his best to keep the ball close to his feet.

Another defender raced over. Kamal put on the brakes, shifted his body right, then went left and turned up the sideline. The defender couldn't stay with him. Kamal burst toward the corner of the box. That's when he spotted Rodrigo on the move. He was open for a crossing pass.

Kamal acted on instinct. He pulled his leg back and fired the ball across the box toward the advancing Rodrigo. Kamal watched and waited. He hoped the pass would go where he intended.

Rodrigo moved toward the ball. But just as he was about to strike it, another Panthers player appeared out of nowhere. It was Justin. He was moving fast into the box. Justin got to the ball and rocketed a kick with his right foot. The goalie never even moved. The kick was a scorcher, fast and strong and aimed at the corner of the goal. The ball sailed past the goalie and into the net.

Justin flung his arms in the air. Rodrigo embraced him. The rest of the Panthers ran over to celebrate with them. Coach Hayes was high-fiving players on the sidelines. The girls who had come to watch Justin were jumping up and down in the bleachers.

Kamal jogged into the mob of players. Some of his teammates high-fived him and congratulated him for his assist. Kamal kept his eye on Justin, who was soaking up the glory of his goal. Kamal wondered if Justin would come over and acknowledge the pass that made his score possible. *Is Justin capable of sharing the spotlight?* Kamal thought. *Can he give someone else credit for his success?* Kamal waited, but Justin didn't approach him. After hugs and high fives with the rest of the team, Justin simply fell back to his spot on the field for the kickoff. Kamal sighed and did the same.

A minute later, the game was over. The Panthers had finally secured their first win of the season. After an on-field celebration and a postgame victory talk from Coach Hayes, the players retreated to the locker room. The noise level was high as the team enjoyed the win. Kamal kept to himself as he changed.

Rodrigo walked over. "Hey, Kamal."

"Hey." Kamal looked up from his spot on a bench.

"Have you said anything to Justin yet?" he asked. They both looked across the locker room. Justin was talking with several players. They were laughing, enjoying their victory.

"No," said Kamal.

"You haven't congratulated him for his goal?" asked Rodrigo.

Kamal scoffed. "He was in the right place at the right time. Anyone could have scored that goal." Kamal began unlacing his cleats.

"Besides, he never even thanked me for the pass. When he thanks me for setting him up for any easy shot, then I'll congratulate him."

"Are you serious?"

"Why not?" asked Kamal.

"Maybe he doesn't know that's what players do in soccer," said Rodrigo. "Maybe he doesn't know you're supposed to thank the guy who assisted you on your goal."

"He's an athlete," said Kamal. "He knows. He just wants to take all the credit."

"Man, I don't know about you sometimes," said Rodrigo. "You need to grow up. Quit worrying about being the Big Dog and all that macho stuff with Justin. Why don't you just be the bigger man and go over there and congratulate him?"

"Him first," said Kamal.

"You guys are something else." Rodrigo shook his head and walked away.

Kamal put his head down and finished unlacing his cleats.

AT practice the next day, spirits were still high. Justin continued to soak up the attention for his game-winning goal, and Kamal kept his distance.

"One on one!" shouted Coach Hayes. "Line it up!" The players jogged over to one of the goals. The goalie moved into the net, and the rest of the team began lining up single file at the edge of the box. Kamal got in line in front of Rodrigo and Justin.

Kamal heard Rodrigo explaining the drill to Justin. "This one's easy," he said. "The first player defends, and the next player tries to score. After you shoot, you immediately become the defender and the guy behind you tries to score."

Kamal waited and watched as the guys in front of him did the drill. He didn't say a word to Rodrigo. He was beginning to get annoyed with how chummy Rodrigo and Justin were getting.

"Great job, guys!" shouted Coach Hayes. "Quick now. Go hard!"

Finally, Kamal was up. He advanced forward with the ball. His defender raced to get into position, but he was too slow. Kamal exploded to the right and got around him easily before firing a shot past the goalie.

"Excellent job, Kamal!" yelled Coach Hayes.

Kamal sprinted back to defend. Rodrigo was coming toward him with the ball. Kamal played it aggressively, thinking he could surprise Rodrigo and go in for a quick tackle. He lunged, diving in at the ball with his left foot. Rodrigo quickly moved the ball backward then spun around Kamal. He tried to recover, but it was too late. Rodrigo was by him. He fired the ball into the goal before Kamal could catch up.

"Great move, Rodrigo!" shouted Coach Hayes.

Kamal returned to his place in line.

Rodrigo quickly got into position on defense. Justin shifted the ball back and forth between his feet. He made a move to the left, but Rodrigo stayed with him, tackling the ball away.

A minute later, Kamal was back up. Again he put a good move on his defender and put the ball into the goal. He was more concerned, however, with stopping Rodrigo on defense. He might not be able to prevent Rodrigo from being friends with Justin, but he could remind him who the Big Dog was on the soccer field.

After his goal, he quickly got into position. Rodrigo broke toward him. Kamal held his ground, keeping low and light on his feet. "Let's go, Rodrigo!" yelled Justin.

"Come on, Kamal!" yelled another player.

Rodrigo took a quick step forward and then stopped. He took another quick step and stopped again. He was trying to get Kamal off balance. It didn't work. When Rodrigo tried the move one last time, Kamal read it. He moved forward the instant Rodrigo stopped with the ball. Rodrigo tried to protect it, but Kamal was there. He kicked the ball away and off the field.

Some of the players cheered. "Way to stay patient!" yelled Coach Hayes.

Kamal felt a surge of pride as he ran to the back of the line.

On Justin's turn on offense, he made some solid moves against Rodrigo and then used his big body to protect the ball. He was beginning to master the finer points of the game. But even with his improved play, Justin was still no match for Rodrigo's defense. Rodrigo tackled the ball cleanly away. "Nice play," said Justin.

"Good effort," said Rodrigo.

After a successful stop on defense, Justin got in line behind Rodrigo. Kamal heard the two of them talking behind him. "Switch with me?" Justin asked. Kamal glanced backward and saw them trading places in line. Kamal knew what that meant. Justin was switching spots because he wanted to face Kamal head-to-head. Kamal smiled. *Any day of the week, California*, he thought.

The players in front of them continued with the drill. Kamal prepared himself mentally as he waited his turn. He couldn't wait to face off against Justin.

When it was Kamal's turn with the ball he danced with it, bouncing on his feet. When his defender leaned a little to the left, Kamal went right, flying toward the goal and blasting a shot past the goalie.

Time to defend. *Let's do this*, he thought.

Justin dribbled toward him.

"Let's go, guys!" shouted Rodrigo. "Go hard!"

Justin kept the ball close to his feet. Kamal hesitated to dive for it. He didn't want to put himself out of position. Then Justin went left and Kamal saw his opportunity. He poked at the ball with his right foot, sending it to the outside and away from Justin. *Yes!* He thought.

"Keep going!" shouted Coach Hayes. "The ball's still in play!"

They both sprinted for the ball. Justin got there first. He controlled the ball, his back to Kamal. Kamal tried jabbing at it, but Justin fended him off with his body. Justin's frame was big, and his body was strong. Kamal continued to kick at the ball, but Justin protected it and used his strength to keep Kamal behind him.

Suddenly Justin turned. Kamal, frustrated, lunged aggressively at the ball and missed. Justin took advantage and dribbled away. Kamal was beaten. Justin approached the goal and blasted a shot low and into the net.

"Yes!" shouted Justin. He ran back and stopped in front of Kamal. "Good effort, man. I can't believe I scored on you." He smiled and set up on defense.

Is he actually trying to be nice to me now? Kamal thought as returned to the end of the line. Once again, Justin had gotten the better of him. And once again, Kamal had no idea how to handle it.

THE next two days at school, Kamal kept
mostly to himself. In physics he was quiet and
sat in the back, several rows from Rodrigo and
Justin. He didn't even have a question for Mr.
Nguyen on Friday. At lunch he ate by himself,
as far away as he could get from Justin.

He and Rodrigo barely spoke, and Kamal
didn't think that bothered Rodrigo. He and
Justin had become fast friends. It seemed that
Rodrigo didn't really need Kamal anymore.

At practice on Friday, Kamal focused on
soccer and tried not to worry about anything
else. Justin could be the cool guy who everyone
liked. Rodrigo and Justin could be best friends.
Whatever. He tried to tell himself that none of
that mattered. What mattered was playing hard,

winning soccer games, and getting to State.

Coach Hayes ran them through their usual drills before dividing the players up for a scrimmage. "Red versus blue!" he barked. "Play hard, just like it's a game. End practice strong and I'll let you all out of here at four thirty to get an early start on your weekend."

The players laughed and cheered and ran to their positions. Kamal and Justin were on the red team. Rodrigo was on blue.

Justin approached Kamal and reached out for a fist bump. Kamal just looked at him. "Come on, man," said Justin. "We're on the same team. Let's go out there and take it to them."

Kamal just looked away.

"Kamal, I'm a competitive guy," said Justin. "So are you. I know we've gotten after each other a few times. If I did anything that crossed the line and upset you, I'm sorry. I want to be your teammate. And I wouldn't mind being your friend too."

"Let's just play this scrimmage and see how it goes," Kamal said. He ran to the opposite sideline, leaving Justin standing alone.

The blue team dominated play early, passing the ball back and forth and keeping it in the red end. Rodrigo made a couple nice moves on his defender and then sent a crossing pass into the box. One of his teammates controlled the ball and took a shot on goal. The goalie for the red team knocked it down with both hands and collected it before a player from blue could pounce on the rebound.

Kamal and his teammates got the ball back but could do little with it. Kamal dribbled the ball up the middle of the field and totally ignored Justin, who was open near midfield on the right. He took it himself but had the ball tackled away by a defender.

"Pass the ball, red!" shouted Coach Hayes. "Justin was open!"

Kamal retreated on defense. Again Rodrigo set up a teammate for a quality scoring opportunity and again the red goalie was forced to make an impressive save. "Nice try!" shouted Rodrigo. "Let's get it back!"

Kamal dribbled the ball forward and tried to thread the needle between two defenders rather than making the easy pass to Justin along the right. He lost the ball again and got tripped up, landing in the grass.

"Kamal!" yelled Coach Hayes. "Pass the ball. Enough with the fancy stuff!"

Rodrigo and his teammates moved quickly the other way. After clearing a couple defenders, Rodrigo and two of his teammates closed in on the goal. Rodrigo passed the ball into the box, then sprinted forward and got it back from his teammate. He made the most of his opportunity, sending the ball hard into the net.

"Nice!" shouted Coach Hayes. "Great teamwork, blue!"

The rest of the scrimmage continued the same way. The blue team played strong, working together and sharing the ball, but Kamal refused to collaborate with Justin. Kamal passed it to other players or made runs himself rather than try to get Justin involved. In the end, blue defeated red, 3–0.

"Let's call it a day," said Coach Hayes. "Red, you have some work to do. Blue, nice job. Everyone, pick up the gear!"

"Hey, Coach Hayes!" yelled Justin. "Some of us want to keep playing. Can we use the small goals? We'll put them away when we're finished."

"Of course," said Coach Hayes.

"Who's in?" shouted Rodrigo. "Who wants to stay and play another scrimmage?" He and Justin were standing together.

Several guys joined them. Others began walking toward the school. "We could use a couple more!" said Justin.

Kamal gathered his gear and began walking away. He rarely turned down a game, but he didn't want to hang out with Justin any more than he had to.

"Kamal!" shouted Rodrigo. "Join us!"

Kamal looked over his shoulder. "Nah. That's all right." He kept walking.

Rodrigo ran up to him. "What's going on?" he asked. "You should play with us."

"I need to get home."

"What for?" Rodrigo got in front of him, forcing Kamal to stop walking. "Stay. I haven't talked to you in days. I miss you, man."

"Sorry, I've got to go."

Kamal started walking. Again Rodrigo moved in front of him. "Kamal. What's going on? Is this about Justin? Is that why you're acting this way?"

Kamal stopped and looked him in the eyes. "I don't know why you like that guy."

Rodrigo laughed. "The two of you need to put this dumb rivalry behind you. Justin is cool. You'd like him if you just gave him a chance. And he'd like you too. You're both just way too competitive for your own good."

"Whatever," said Kamal. "You go play with your new best friend. I'm out of here."

Kamal hitched his bag up around his shoulders and headed toward the school.

KAMAL remained in a funk throughout the weekend. He kept to himself, spending most of the time holed up in his bedroom. Rodrigo tried reaching out to him several times, but Kamal ignored his phone calls and text messages. He didn't want to talk to Rodrigo. He didn't see the point.

Monday afternoon the Panthers took the road to play a game against the Trout River Whitefish. As Kamal and Rodrigo got ready to take the field, Justin walked over. "Good luck, Rodrigo," he said. "You too, Kamal."

"Thanks," said Rodrigo. Kamal ignored him.

"Let's go, Panthers!" shouted Coach Hayes as the two teams got ready for the kickoff.

"Play hard, everyone!" shouted Rodrigo.

Justin started the game on the sideline. "Put the pressure on them right away!" he yelled from the bench.

Kamal remained quiet. He just wanted to play. He wanted to take all his frustration and pent-up energy and use it against the Whitefish. He would let his feet do the talking.

As soon as the game began, Kamal controlled the ball. He attempted a long run up the sideline. "Open!" shouted Rodrigo in the middle of the field. Kamal looked at him but kept the ball. A Trout River player tackled it away just seconds later.

On the Panthers' next possession, Kamal received the pass from a teammate and again tried to take over the game by himself. "Left!" shouted a teammate. Instead of passing, Kamal dribbled up the middle of the field and tried to get past three Whitefish defenders. They closed on him and easily cleared the ball away.

"Teamwork!" shouted Coach Hayes. "Pass the ball!"

Finally, the Panthers had an opening. Some of Kamal's teammates controlled the ball behind him at midfield. He and the other Panthers forwards jockeyed for position near the Whitefish goal.

Rodrigo got the ball along the right side and dribbled toward the corner. Kamal moved in that direction, setting up in the box to receive the pass. Rodrigo protected the ball as two defenders came over to stop him. He quickly moved to the end line as one of the Whitefish defenders dove in and tackled the ball out of bounds. Rodrigo had forced an early corner kick.

Kamal set up in the box. Rodrigo joined him. A Panthers' forward set up for the corner. Normally on a corner kick, Kamal and Rodrigo would take charge, talking to each other and telling the other players where to go. But Kamal remained silent. He didn't even look at Rodrigo as he walked to the opposite end of the box.

The kick came in. It sailed high and began bending tightly toward the net. Kamal wanted the goal. He eyed the ball and then went for it. He darted into the middle of the box and pushed off the ground for the header. Unfortunately, so did Rodrigo. Their legs got tangled up, and both of them went crashing to the turf. The ball flew through the box and was taken by a Whitefish defender.

Rodrigo got to his feet and extended a hand to Kamal. Kamal ignored it. He stood up on his own and jogged away to play defense.

"Talk to each other out there!" yelled Coach Hayes.

The Whitefish moved the ball in the other direction. Kamal and his teammates scrambled back to defend the counterattack. A pass went deep into the Panthers' zone. A Whitefish player tracked it down and immediately made a pass to a teammate streaking toward the goal.

The Whitefish forward got the ball in stride, went around a Panthers' defender, and was alone in front of the goal. The Panthers' goalie slid along the grass, hoping to punch the ball out, but the Whitefish player was too quick. He danced around the diving tackle and waltzed in for the easy goal. The Whitefish had an early 1–0 lead.

"Let's go, Panthers!" shouted Rodrigo as the teams lined up for the kickoff.

"No problem!" yelled Justin from the sideline. "There's a lot of game left!"

The half continued with neither team mounting another major threat. Kamal tried to make several long solo runs with the ball and never looked to pass the ball to Rodrigo. He was stopped each time, making Coach Hayes more and more upset with Kamal's lack of teamwork. "Cooperate out there!" he yelled. "Rodrigo's getting open. Come on now!"

With just minutes left in the first half, Kamal waited on the right side as his teammates controlled the ball near midfield. The Panthers made short passes to keep the ball away from Whitefish defenders. Kamal began to grow impatient. He wanted the ball. "Open!" he yelled.

Suddenly one of the Panthers sliced through the defense with the ball near the middle of the field, luring a defender toward him. He then dumped the ball off to a teammate on the right. Rodrigo made a couple quick steps to get open. His teammate found him, delivering a pass on target. Rodrigo trapped it and kept his back to his defender, shielding him from the ball. He dribbled the ball away, trying to give himself a little room.

"Right!" shouted Kamal. He was wide open for a crossing pass.

Rodrigo turned with the ball and looked up. He saw Kamal but then immediately looked away. Instead he found a teammate at the top of the box. Rodrigo stepped to his right and delivered the pass.

Rodrigo moved without the ball, faking to the outside before cutting inside. His teammate found him in the box and delivered a pass. Rodrigo trapped the ball with his chest, keeping his back to the goal.

Kamal darted toward the box. "Open!" he screamed.

Instead of passing, Rodrigo took it

himself. He quickly turned, found the space he needed, and fired a shot on goal. It rose high and to the left, narrowly missing the outstretched fingers of the goalie and sailing into the net. Rodrigo had tied the game.

The Panthers mobbed Rodrigo, but Kamal didn't join the celebration. He was too upset that his so-called friend had refused to pass him the ball.

Seconds later, the referee blew his whistle, ending the first half.

The Panthers made their way to the sideline. Kamal ran up to Rodrigo. "I was open the whole time," he said.

"Thanks for congratulating me on my goal," said Rodrigo sarcastically.

"Why didn't you pass it to me?"

"Are you serious?" asked Rodrigo. "You're like a black hole out there. Once you get the ball you never give it back. You're playing like a selfish child. Besides, I scored, didn't I?"

Kamal didn't want to hear any more. He turned his back and began to walk away.

"You're not the team player you used to be," said Rodrigo. "And I'm not the only one who thinks so. Lots of the guys have been saying the same thing."

Kamal stopped and turned. "Is that right?"

"If this team has any shot of going to State, we need your leadership," said Rodrigo.

"So now I'm not a leader, either? Is that what you're saying?"

"I know this is about Justin," said Rodrigo. "I know you don't like the guy. But your jealousy for him is getting the better of you. It's becoming ridiculous. It's hurting the team."

"I told you already," said Kamal. "I'm not jealous."

"And another thing," said Rodrigo. "Just because you don't like Justin doesn't mean you have to be a jerk to me. I thought we were friends."

"Me too," said Kamal. "Before you started taking Justin's side."

"You know what? I'm done," said Rodrigo. "I'm over this." He walked toward the sideline, leaving Kamal standing alone.

THE game remained tied for most of the second half. Kamal never once passed the ball to Rodrigo. Their conversation had made him feel even less willing to cooperate. Every time the ball came to him he was determined to score a goal on his own. He would prove to Rodrigo that he didn't need him.

It didn't work out as he had hoped. The Whitefish defense figured out that Kamal was easy to defend because he never passed the ball. They threw two or three defenders at him each time, easily tackling the ball away.

"Teamwork!" shouted Coach Hayes.

"Pass the ball!" screamed a fed up Rodrigo.

After another attempted run up the middle, a Trout River player easily took the ball away from Kamal at midfield and cleared it back to a fellow defender along the sideline. Kamal chased the ball, desperately wanting it back for another scoring chance. The Whitefish player trapped the pass and controlled it. Kamal sprinted toward him, but he was moving too fast. His positioning was terrible. The Whitefish player made a simple move to his right and sent the ball wide to a teammate on the near side. Kamal's momentum took him past the Whitefish player and put him wildly out of position.

"Kamal, get back!" shouted Coach Hayes.

Kamal made a lackluster attempt to join his teammates on defense. The Whitefish player on the near side lofted a long pass down the line, leading a teammate into the corner. The Panthers scrambled backward into their own end, but it was too late. The Trout River player made a quick crossing pass into the box that was met perfectly by a teammate. He drilled a header past the Panthers' goalie and into the net. Trout River celebrated while the Panthers hung their heads in disappointment.

As the teams moved into position for the kickoff, Kamal heard Coach Hayes from the sideline. "Sub!" Kamal looked over. Coach Hayes was putting Justin into the game. Kamal just shook his head.

Justin ran toward him. "Kamal!" he shouted.

"What?" Kamal asked.

"You're out," said Justin. "Coach Hayes is putting me in."

"No way." Kamal didn't believe him. "You must've heard Coach Hayes wrong."

"Sorry," said Justin. "I wish we could play together, but that's what Coach said."

"You have got to be kidding me," said Kamal.

Rodrigo jogged over. "You're out," he said. "Hurry up. Get off the field."

"This has to be some kind of a joke," said Kamal.

"Kamal!" yelled Coach Hayes, waving him over. "Let's go!"

The referee ran in. "Is there a problem here?"

"No problem, sir," said Rodrigo. "Just some confusion on the substitution."

"All right," said the ref. "Get it figured out. Let's get going."

Rodrigo glared at Kamal.

Kamal shook his head and finally gave in. "Unbelievable." He made a point of bumping into Justin on his way off the field.

"Let's go, Panthers!" shouted Rodrigo behind him. "Let's get a goal back!"

Coach Hayes met Kamal on the sideline. "You're better than this," he said. "We play as a team. Never forget that."

"Whatever," said Kamal as he sat down.

"Check the attitude, Kamal," said Coach Hayes. "Watch yourself."

Kamal took a drink and then slammed his water bottle to the ground. He leaned backward and placed a towel over his head.

The game continued without him. With only a few minutes to go, the Panthers needed a goal just to secure the tie.

Rodrigo became the team's general, barking out orders and leading them down the field. "Great job, Rodrigo!" shouted Coach Hayes.

Justin had the ball along the right side.

As a defender approached him, he passed to Rodrigo at midfield. Rodrigo had room to operate and streaked toward the Whitefish goal. Justin ran with him. Rodrigo made a quick move, sidestepping a defender and dribbling toward the left-hand corner of the box. Before two Trout River defenders could get to him, Rodrigo passed the ball to Justin, who was at the top of the box. Justin had just enough room to get off a shot. He planted his foot and put all his weight behind the ball. The shot was a rocket, and it was positioned perfectly. It sailed through the defense and past the goalie. Justin's shot found the corner of the net.

Rodrigo ran over to him and jumped into his arms. The other Panthers joined the celebration. Kamal didn't even stand up.

Following the kickoff, the Panthers tried their best to get another goal, but time ran out. The game ended in a 2–2 tie.

Kamal remained on the sideline as his teammates gathered together on the field. He watched their high fives and hugs and noticed smiles on the faces of most of the players. They were celebrating and having a good time, which in Kamal's opinion was the wrong way to act after a tie game. You celebrate wins, not ties.

As the two teams shook hands on the field, Coach Hayes approached him. "Is this how you're planning on acting from now on?"

Kamal said nothing.

"Because it's unacceptable for me." Coach Hayes sat down next to him. "Kamal, don't think I haven't noticed what's going on. You've become a different player ever since Justin joined the team."

Kamal looked down at his feet.

"I get it," Coach continued. "Justin's got a big personality and a pretty loud mouth. But here's the deal, Kamal. You have to work through this stuff. You have to step up and go back to being the leader this team needs."

Kamal leaned forward. He felt tears welling up in his eyes. "Nobody even wants me out there on the field anymore. The whole team thinks I've failed them. That I've got a bad attitude, that I'm not a team player."

Coach Hayes put his arm on Kamal's back. "You know, I did hear some of the guys talking about that the other day," he said. Coach Hayes paused. "But you know who came to your defense? You know who told the other players they were wrong? Who had nothing but positive things to say about you?"

A tear streaked down Kamal's cheek.

"That's right," said Coach Hayes. "It was Rodrigo. I know this whole thing with Justin has come between you and Rodrigo, but Rodrigo will always have your back. And so will your teammates, if you start trusting them and putting the team first again. What do you think?"

Kamal nodded. "I think you're right."

"Good," said Coach Hayes. "Let's start winning some soccer games." He smiled and walked away.

Kamal stayed on the bench. He felt horrible. How had he managed to screw things up so badly with his teammates and with his best friend? He needed to think. And he needed to fix it.

EVEN though Kamal desperately wanted to apologize to Rodrigo, he avoided him for the next two days. He didn't know what to say. Besides, he had said and done so many things he regretted, he didn't know where to begin. Kamal wondered if a sappy apology would seem hollow and if maybe he didn't really deserve Rodrigo's forgiveness.

Instead Kamal decided he would let his play on the field speak for itself. On Thursday the Panthers were back at home for a game against the Rockway Red Hawks.

During warm-ups, Kamal quietly pushed himself and his teammates, leading the Panthers by example. As the teams set up for the kickoff, beads of sweat were already trickling down his face. He was ready.

Kamal and Rodrigo were in the starting lineup. So was Justin. That didn't bother Kamal. His focus was on making things better with Rodrigo and winning the game. He wasn't concerned with Justin anymore. Plus it made sense that Justin had received a starting spot. He had earned it.

Following the kickoff, the Panthers controlled the play. They held onto the ball for long stretches of time, keeping the Red Hawks on their heels. They were playing with more patience and poise than they had all season. "Protect it!" shouted Kamal as the ball was passed between three Panthers' defenders at midfield.

Suddenly, Kamal saw an opening. Justin received a pass in the middle of the field, about fifteen yards in front of the box. Kamal broke forward, hugging the sideline. He noticed that Rodrigo was moving with him in the center of the field. Kamal raised his arm. Justin spotted him and fed him a clean pass.

The Red Hawks' defense had stayed with Kamal. In fact, three guys were descending on him from three different directions. That left Rodrigo in a one-on-one situation, just steps from the box.

Rodrigo made a break toward the goal. Kamal had just seconds to get rid of the ball before the defense was on top of him. He unleashed the pass. It sailed high and over the head of Rodrigo's defender. Rodrigo raced to meet the pass. He trapped it, dribbled forward, and buried a shot in the net.

Tweet! The referee blew his whistle.

Kamal looked to the sideline. The linesman had his flag in the air, signaling offside. Kamal's pass had been just a split second too late. No goal.

Rodrigo ran back and gave Kamal a thumbs-up. Kamal pumped his fist in return. "Next time!" he yelled.

Play went back and forth for several minutes as both the Panthers and the Red Hawks looked to get on the scoreboard first. "Solid passes!" yelled Kamal. "Play together!"

"Great teamwork, guys!" shouted Rodrigo.

The Panthers defended the ball in their zone and intercepted a Red Hawks' pass.

Immediately they began another charge up the field.

One of Kamal's teammates dribbled the ball up the middle. "Right side!" shouted Kamal. Rodrigo was open on the right, and Kamal wanted to make sure his teammate saw him. The player with the ball heard Kamal's call and passed it to Rodrigo, who began working his way to the Red Hawks' goal.

Kamal eased forward along the left side. Justin was in the middle of the field. "Cross back!" shouted Kamal. Rodrigo dribbled forward and then lofted the ball backward to Justin. Justin immediately spotted Kamal and sent the ball his way. Kamal received the pass and made a quick move around his defender. He was cruising forward along the sideline with plenty of room in front of him to make a play.

His teammates ran with him. Kamal glanced across the field. "Go!" he shouted to Justin. He wanted Justin to push forward and get open in the box. Justin responded and slid around his defender. Kamal made a couple long strides down the sideline then led Justin into the box with a pass along the grass. His pass was a little too hard. Instead of finding Justin's foot it was met by a Red Hawks defender. He tried to clear the ball away, but Justin was there with a high kick to knock it out of the air. He trapped the ball then passed it back to Kamal on the left.

Kamal looked around. The Red Hawks' goalie had shifted over to prevent a shot attempt. That left the right side completely open. Rodrigo was there, in perfect position. Kamal took a couple steps to clear himself from his defender, then he fired the ball through the air, over the defense and across the box.

Rodrigo tapped the ball to the ground with his chest. He controlled it and took a couple steps to his left, looking for an open window. *Nail it*, thought Kamal. *Do it, Rodrigo.*

Rodrigo set himself, then blasted the ball toward the net. It flew past a defender, rose into the air, and found the upper corner of the goal. The goalie never had a chance.

Kamal raced over to congratulate him.

"Way to bury it!" he said, giving Rodrigo a high five.

"Thanks," said Rodrigo. He seemed a little surprised by Kamal's reaction. "Great pass."

Justin ran in. "Nice effort trying to find me."

"Sorry I led you a little too far," said Kamal.

"Kamal?" asked Rodrigo.

"Yeah?"

"Are you okay?" asked Rodrigo.

Kamal just smiled.

Justin grabbed Rodrigo around the neck. "Of course he's okay. We just scored a goal, didn't we?"

"We sure did," said Rodrigo.

The three of them jogged down the field together and got into position for the kickoff. Kamal couldn't stop smiling. He felt good. Really good.

THE first half ended with the Panthers ahead of the Red Hawks, 1–0. The players sat together on the bench, toweling off and drinking water.

"Great play out there," said Coach Hayes. "You're in sync. You're sharing the ball. You're playing unselfishly. You're doing the things great teams do." He paced back and forth in front of them. "Now let's pick up the pressure in the second half. Don't be afraid to go after the ball and press forward a little more on defense. You can do it. Let's get this win!"

The players cheered and got to their feet. Kamal took one last swig of water. He threw his bottle and his towel to the ground and began walking onto the field. Suddenly, Rodrigo was next to him.

"Hey," he said.

Kamal stopped walking. "Hey."

Rodrigo smiled. "You want to tell me what's going on?"

"What are you talking about?" asked Kamal.

"You, and the way you're playing," said Rodrigo. "You're actually passing the ball. And saying nice things to people."

"It's the new and improved Kamal, I guess."

"Actually you seem like the old Kamal if you ask me," said Rodrigo. "The one I used to really like."

"I'm playing the way I should have been playing all along," said Kamal. "Like a teammate. I've been acting like a complete idiot. To Justin, to you, to everybody."

"I can't disagree with that," said Rodrigo.

"Hey!" said Kamal. "I'm trying to say I'm sorry here."

Rodrigo grinned. "So are you planning to give this same speech to Justin?"

"Let's not go that far." They both laughed. "Can you accept my apology for the way I've been acting lately?"

"Of course," said Rodrigo.

"Friends?" asked Kamal. He stuck out his hand.

"We always were," said Rodrigo, gripping Kamal's hand firmly.

Kamal looked out to the field. "All right, then. Let's get out there and win this thing."

The Panthers came out strong in the second half, following Coach Hayes's orders by pushing forward more on defense. Unfortunately, the Red Hawks came out even stronger. They took advantage of the Panthers' aggressive defense and mounted several scoring attacks. They finally struck pay dirt after Kamal barely missed a tackle and the player he was defending launched the ball deep into the Panthers' end. A Red Hawk dribbled the ball forward then hit a teammate in stride streaking toward the net. His shot was on target, tying the game, 1–1.

"No problem!" shouted Rodrigo. "We'll get it back!"

Kamal nodded at him. "Come on, guys! Keep up the aggressive play!"

Minutes ticked off the clock as the teams exchanged scoring chances. The Panthers were clicking. Their passes were sharp and their spacing was dead on. They were doing everything right except putting the ball into the net. The Red Hawks' goalie managed to dive and stretch and lunge, preventing each of the Panthers' shots from hitting its mark.

As the Panthers set up for a goal kick, Kamal and Rodrigo tried to keep their teammates engaged. With just minutes remaining in the game, it was now or never. "Keep pushing, guys!" shouted Rodrigo.

"Let's attack!" yelled Kamal. "Play smart."

The goal kick came in high. Several players behind Kamal jockeyed for position to control it. A Red Hawks' player was under the ball, but suddenly Justin exploded in front of him and used his strength to steal it away. He quickly cleared the ball to a teammate on the far side.

"Great play, Justin!" shouted Kamal. He began easing his way forward along the side.

Panthers defenders controlled the ball for several minutes. They took turns with it, passing it back and forth and waiting patiently for someone to get open in front of them.

"Come on, guys," said Kamal. "There's not a lot of time." He loved his teammates' willingness to wait for the right moment to strike, but he knew that time was running out. They didn't have all day.

Suddenly, Kamal heard a cry go out from a teammate. "Open!" A Panther was sprinting across the field, into a gap in the middle, just across the centerline. It was Justin. He received the pass and kept charging down the field. Kamal moved forward, looking to get open for Justin. He could see Rodrigo doing the same on the other side.

Justin stopped in front of the box, his back to the goal. As two Red Hawks' defenders descended on him, Justin did to them what he had done to Kamal in practice several days ago. He used his big shoulders and his strong hips to keep both defenders behind him and to prevent them from getting the ball. He then turned and spotted Rodrigo open on the far side. Justin planted his foot and sent a long pass his direction.

Justin's pass was perfect. Rodrigo knocked the ball down with his right foot and dribbled forward. The Red Hawks' defense shifted toward the ball.

Suddenly Kamal's closest defender was ten yards away. He thought about shouting to Rodrigo, but he didn't want to draw attention to himself. Rodrigo would find him. When he did, Kamal would be all alone for the shot.

Kamal was right. Rodrigo glanced his way for just a split second, and that was all it took. He cleared himself from his defender and fired a crossing pass toward Kamal. The defense scrambled to shift back. Kamal took the pass and dribbled hard to the goal.

Kamal had a shot, but the goalie was quickly moving to cut off the angle. That's when Kamal spotted a player out of the corner of his eye. It was Rodrigo, and no one was defending him.

Kamal dribbled closer to the net, drawing the goalie further to his side. When he knew the goalie was too far to get back, Kamal passed the ball to Rodrigo's waiting foot. All Rodrigo had to do was poke at it gently and direct it easily into the goal.

Kamal ran over to Rodrigo. Along with Justin and the rest of their teammates, they mobbed together in a huge group hug. "Great pass!" said Rodrigo.

"Same to you," said Kamal.

"I'm starting to like this sport," said Justin. Kamal and Rodrigo laughed.

The game ended in a 2–1 victory for the Panthers. Kamal immediately found Rodrigo and Justin. "Now that's what I call teamwork."

"I think we finally got this train back on its tracks," said Rodrigo.

"Let's take it all the way to the playoffs!" said Kamal. "And then to State!"

Justin gave him a high five. "That works for me!"

"Justin," said Kamal with a smile. "You're not too bad for a lacrosse player."

"Why thank you," said Justin taking a bow.

"You're so good in fact that you've got me thinking." Kamal stroked his chin. "I might go out for the lacrosse team this spring. If you can become a killer soccer player this quickly, I'm sure I could learn how to play lacrosse just as fast."

"Lacrosse is a much more complicated sport," Justin said.

"Rodrigo?" said Kamal. "Are you hearing what I'm hearing? I think our friend Justin here is doubting my athletic ability." He smiled at Rodrigo.

Rodrigo nodded. "I think you're right," he said. "I think you should go out for lacrosse, Kamal. I think you'd be really good. I might just join you."

Justin looked back and forth between them. Kamal and Rodrigo broke out laughing.

"Ah, I get it," said Justin. "You're messing with me."

"I don't know a thing about lacrosse," said Kamal. "Heck, I don't even know what that stick thing is called."

"It's called a stick," said Justin.

"Makes sense," said Rodrigo.

Kamal's eyes went wide. "What a complicated sport," he joked. They all laughed.

They jogged toward their teammates, who were lining up for postgame handshakes.

"The win feels good," said Justin.

"Not as good as the next one," said Kamal. "I sense a winning streak in our future."

"I like the sound of that!" shouted Rodrigo.

The three of them blended in with their teammates and began shaking hands with the Red Hawks. Kamal let out a big, deep breath. His senior year had become much more complicated than he had expected. But things were better than ever now, and the real season had just begun.

GRIDIRON

THE CLUTCH
PAUL HOBLIN

THE EXTRA POINT
CHRIS KREIE

FALSE START
PAUL HOBLIN

THE LATE HIT
K. R. COLEMAN

SHOWDOWN
K. R. COLEMAN

SIGNING DAY
K. R. COLEMAN

Leave it all on the field!

STEP UP YOUR GAME

ABOUT THE AUTHOR

Chris Kreie is an elementary school teacher in Eden Prairie, Minnesota. He's an avid sports fan and outdoorsman who especially enjoys hiking and camping near Lake Superior along Minnesota's north shore. He lives in Minneapolis with his wife and two children.